Ginger and the Kingsmarkham Chalk Circle

RUTH RENDELL

Contents

A Phoenix Paperback

Ginger and the Kingsmarkham Chalk Circle and
May and June by Ruth Rendell are included in
Ruth Rendell's *Collected Short Stories*, published by Hutchinson

This edition published in 1996 by Phoenix
a division of Orion Books Ltd
Orion House, 5 Upper St Martin's Lane, London WC2H 9EA

ISBN 1 85799 745 X

Typeset by Deltatype Ltd, Ellesmere Port, Cheshire
Printed in Great Britain by Clays Ltd, St Ives plc

Ginger and the Kingsmarkham
Chalk Circle

'There's a girl downstairs, sir,' said Polly Davies, 'and she says somone's taken her baby out of its pram.'

Chief Inspector Wexford had been contemplating a sheet of foolscap. On it, written by himself in the cause of crime prevention, was a politely worded request to the local authority, asking them to refrain from erecting scaffolding around their rented property a full nine months before building work was due to commence. Because of the scaffolding there had already been two burglaries and an assault on a young woman. He looked up from the paper, adjusted his thoughts and sighed.

'They will do it,' he said. 'Leave their babies about I mean. You'd never find them leaving their handbags outside shops.'

'It was outside her flat, sir, not a shop, and the thing is, whoever took the baby left another one in its place.'

Slowly Wexford got up. He came round the desk and looked narrowly at Polly.

'Constable Davies, you have to be pulling my leg.'

'No, sir, you know I wouldn't. She's a Mrs Bond and she

says that when she went downstairs to fetch in her pram, her baby had gone and another one been put there.'

Wexford followed Polly down to the ground floor. In one of the interview rooms a girl was sitting at the bleak, rectangular, plastic-topped table, drinking tea and crying. She looked about nineteen. She had long straw-coloured hair and a small childish face, naive and innocent and frightened, and she was wearing blue denims and a tee-shirt with apples and oranges and cherries printed all over the front. From her appearance one would not have supposed her to be a mother. But also in the room was a baby. The baby, in short white frock and woolly coat and napkin and cotton socks, slept in the uneasy arms of Detective Constable Loring.

It had occurred to Wexford on the way down that women who have recently had babies are, or are said to be, prone to various kinds of mental disturbance, and his first thought was that Mrs Bond might only think or only be saying that this child was not hers.

'Now, Mrs Bond,' he began, 'this is a strange business. Do you feel like telling me about it?'

'I've told it all,' she said.

'Well, yes, but not to me. Why not start by telling me where you live and where your baby was?'

She gulped. She pushed the teacup away. 'Greenhill Court. We're on the fifth floor. We haven't got a balcony or anything. I have to go all the way down in the lift to put Karen out in her pram. She's got to have fresh air. And when she's there I can't watch her all the time. I can't even see her from my lounge on account of it looks out over the car park.'

'So you put her out in the pram this afternoon,' said Wexford. 'What time would that have been?'

'It was just on two. I put the pram on the grass with the cat net on it, and when I went to fetch it in at half-past four the cat net was still on it and the baby was asleep but it – it wasn't Karen!' She made little whimpering noises that exploded in a sob. 'It wasn't Karen, it was that baby he's holding!'

The baby woke up and also began to cry. Loring wrinkled up his nose and shifted his left hand from under its buttocks. His eyes appealed to Polly who nodded and left the room.

'So what did you do?' said Wexford.

'I didn't even go back upstairs. I got hold of the pram and I pushed it and I started to run and I ran all the way down here to you.'

He was touched by her childish faith. In real or imaginary trouble, at time of fear, she ran to those whom her sheltered small-town upbringing had taught her to trust, the kindly helmeted man in blue, the strong arm of the law. Not for her the grosser cynical image her city-bred contemporaries held of brutal and bribable policemen.

'Mrs Bond,' he said, and then, 'What's your first name?'

'Philippa. I'm called Pippa.'

'Then I'll call you that if you don't mind. Describe your baby to me, will you, Pippa? Is she dark or fair? How old is she?'

'She's two months old – well, nine weeks. She's got blue eyes, she's wearing a white frock.' The voice broke and trembled again. 'And she's got the most beautiful red-gold hair you've ever seen!'

Inevitably, Wexford's eyes went to the child in Loring's arms whom this description seemed perfectly to fit. He said gently to Pippa Bond, 'Now you're quite sure you aren't imagining all this? No one will be angry if you are, we shall understand. Perhaps you worried or felt a bit guilty about leaving Karen out of your sight for so long, and then when you came down you got a feeling she looked rather different from usual and . . .'

A wail of indignation and misery cut across the rest of what he had to say. The girl began to cry with long tearing sobs. Polly Davies came back, carrying a small square hand towel from the women's lavatory. She took the baby from Loring, laid it on its back on the table and undid the big safety pin above its navel. Pippa Bond flinched away from the baby as if it were carrying a disease.

'I'm not imagining it,' she shouted at Wexford. 'I'm not! D'you think I wouldn't know my own baby? D'you think I wouldn't know my Karen from *that*?'

Polly had folded the towel cornerwise. She moved a little so that Wexford could see the baby's waving legs and bare crotch. 'Whoever this baby is, sir, it isn't Karen. Look for yourself – it's a boy.'

Trevor Bond was fetched from the Stowerton estate agent's where he worked. He looked very little older than his wife.

Pippa clung to him, crying and inarticulate, and over her bent head he cast despairing eyes at the policemen.

He had arrived in a car driven by a young woman he said was his sister-in-law, Pippa's sister, who also lived at Greenhill Court with her husband. She sat stiffly at the wheel, giving Pippa no more than a nod and what seemed like a shrug of exasperation when she came out of the police station with Trevor's arm round her. Susan Rains, her name was, and a quarter of an hour later it was she who was showing Loring and Sergeant Martin just where the pram had stood on the lawn between the block of flats and the main road from Kingsmarkham to Stowerton. While this thin red-haired girl castigated her sister's negligence and put forward her own theories as to where Karen might be, Dr Moss arrived with sedation for Pippa, though she had become calmer once she understood no one would expect her to have charge of the changeling boy.

His fate was removal to a Kingsmarkham Borough nursery for infants in the care of the local authority.

'Poor lamb,' said the children's officer Wexford spoke to. 'I expect Kay will be able to take him in Bystall Lane. There's no one to fetch him, though, they've got ten to bath and get to bed down there.'

Young Ginger, Wexford had begun to call him. He was a fine-looking baby with large eyes, strong pudgy features, and hair of a curious pale red, the colour of a new raw carrot. To Wexford's not inexperienced eye, he looked older than the missing Karen, nearer four months than two. His eyes were able to focus firmly, and now they focused on the chief inspector, a scrutiny which moved the baby to yell miserably. Young Ginger buried his face in Polly's boyish bosom, crying and searching for sustenance.

'You don't know what they're thinking, do you, sir?' Polly said. 'Just because we can't remember anything about when we were his age we sort of think babies don't feel much or notice things. But suppose what they feel is so awful they sort of block it off just so as they won't be able to remember? Suppose it's dreadful pain being separated from your mother and not being able to say and – Oh, I don't know, but does anyone think of these things, sir?'

'Well, psychiatrists do,' said Wexford, 'and philosophers, I expect, but not many ordinary people like us. You'll have to remember it when you have babies of your own. Now take him down to Bystall Lane, will you?'

A few minutes after she had gone Inspector Burden came in. He had heard the story downstairs but had not entirely believed it. It was the part about putting another baby in Karen's place that he couldn't believe, he told Wexford. He hadn't either, said Wexford, but it was true.

'You can't think of a reason why anyone would do such a thing,' said Burden. 'You can't think of a single reason why even a mentally disturbed person would do such a thing.'

'I suppose,' said Wexford, 'that by "you" you mean yourself or "one" because *I* can think of several reasons for doing it. First of all, you've got to take some degree of mental disturbance for granted here. Well-adjusted normal people don't steal other people's babies, let alone exchange them. It's going to be a woman. It's a woman who's done it because she wants to be rid of that particular child, yet she must have a child. Agreed?'

'Right,' said Burden. 'Why?'

'She has to show it to someone else,' Wexford said slowly, as if thinking aloud, 'someone who expects to see a baby nearer in age and appearance to Karen Bond than to young Ginger, or who expects a baby of Karen's sex. She may be a woman who has several sons and whose husband was away when the last one was born. She has told him he has a daughter, and to bear this out because she's afraid of him, she has to have a girl to produce for him. On the other hand, she may not be married. She may have told a boy friend or ex-boy friend the child is younger than it is in order to convince him of his paternity.'

'I'm glad you mentioned mental disturbance,' said Burden sarcastically.

'She may simply be exhausted by looking after a child who screams incessantly – young Ginger's got a good pair of lungs – so she exchanges him for a baby she believes won't scream. Or she may have been told that Ginger has some illness or even hereditary defect which frightened her so she wanted to be rid of him, but she still has to have a baby for her husband or mother or whoever to see.'

Burden seemed to be considering this inventiveness with reluctant admiiration but not much conviction. He said, 'So what are we going to do about it?'

'I've taken everyone in the place off what they were doing and put them on to this. We're getting on to all the hospitals and GPs, the Registrar of births, and the post-natal and baby clinics. I think it has to be someone local, maybe even someone who knew the pram would be there because she'd seen it there before.'

'And seen the baby who was in it before?' asked Burden, quirking up an eyebrow.

'Not necessarily. A pram with a cat net over and whose occupant can't be seen implies a very young baby.' Wexford hesitated. 'This is a hell of a lot more worrying,' he said, 'than a run-of-the-mill baby-snatching.'

'Because Karen Bond's so young?' Burden hazarded.

'No, not that. Look, Mike, your typical baby-snatcher loves babies, she yearns for one of her own, and that's why she takes someone else's. But this one's *got* a baby of her own and one she dislikes enough to hand him over to a stranger. You can pretty well take it for granted the ordinary baby-snatcher will care for a child almost extravagantly well, but will this one? If she doesn't care for her own child, will she care for a substitute? I say it's worrying because we can be certain this woman's taken Karen for a purpose, a use, and what happens when that use is over?'

The block of flats in which the Bonds lived was not one of those concerning whose vulnerability to break-ins Wexford had been drafting his letter, but a privately owned five-storeyed building standing on what not long ago had been open green meadows. There were three such blocks, Greenhill, Fairlawn and Hillside Courts, interspersed with rows of weatherboarded town houses, and each block was separated from the main road to Stowerton only by a strip of lawn thirty feet deep. On this turf, a little way in from the narrow service road, Karen Bond's pram had stood.

Wexford and Burden talked to the porter who had charge of the three blocks. He had been cleaning a car in the car park at the relevant time and had noticed nothing. Wexford, going up in the Greenhill lift, commented to Burden that it was unfortunate children were forbidden to play on the lawns. They would have served as protection for Karen or at least as witnesses. There were a good many children on this new estate which was mainly occupied by young couples. Between two and four-thirty that afternoon the little ones had been cooped up in small rooms or out for walks with their mothers, the older ones at school.

Mrs Louise Pelham had fetched her son and her next-door neighbour's two sons home from school, passing within a few feet of Karen's pram. That was at a quarter to four. She had glanced into the pram, as she always did, and now she said she remembered thinking Karen looked 'funny'. The baby in the pram had seemed to have a bigger face and redder hair than the one she had looked at when she passed on her way to the children's school half an hour before. Wexford felt that there was a real lead here, a pinpointing of the time of the substitution, until he learned that Susan Rains had been with Mrs Pelham before him and told her the whole story in detail.

Susan Rains and her sister Pippa had each been married at the age of eighteen, but Pippa at twenty already had a baby while Susan, seven years older, was childless. She was without a job too, it appeared, and at three years short of thirty was leading the life of a middle-aged houseproud gossip. She seemed very anxious to tell Wexford and Burden that, in her opinion, her sister was far too young to have a child, her brother-in-law too young to be a father, and that they were both too irresponsible to look after the baby. Pippa, she said, was always bringing Karen round for her to mind, and now Wexford, who had been wondering about the two folded napkins, the plastic spoon and bottle of concentrated orange juice on Mrs Rains's spotless kitchen counter, understood why they were there.

'Are you fond of babies, Mrs Rains?' Wexford asked, and got an almost frightening response.

Hard lines bit into Mrs Rains's face and her redhead's pale eyes flashed. 'I'd be an unnatural woman if I wasn't, wouldn't I?' What else she might have said – a defence? An explanation? – was cut off by the arrival of a woman in her late forties whom she introduced in a mutter as her mother. It was left to Wexford to find out that this was Mrs Leighton who had left Pippa in a drugged sleep and Trevor trying to answer Sergeant Martin's second spate of questions.

Mrs Leighton was sprightly and not too concerned. 'Well, babies that get taken out of prams, they always turn up safe and sound, don't they?' Her hair was dyed to a more glorious red than her daughter's natural shade. She was on her way to babysit for her son and daughter-in-law who had a six-month-old son, and she had just looked in on Pippa to collect the one pound twenty she owed her for dry-cleaning. Imagine what she'd felt, the whole place full of policemen and Karen gone. She really thought Trevor or Susan might have phoned her, and now she was in two minds whether to go and babysit for Mark or not. 'But she's bound to turn up OK, isn't she?' she said to Wexford.

Wexford said they must hope so, and then he and Burden left the two women to argue between themselves as to which was the more important, keeping a promise to the son or commiserating with the daughter.

The world, or this small corner of it, suddenly seemed full of babies. From behind two doors on the ground floor came the whimpers and low peevish grizzlings of infants put unwillingly in their cots for the night. As they left by the glass double doors, they passed on the step an athletic-looking girl in sweater and demins with a very small baby clamped to her chest in a canvas baby carrier. The car park was filling as men returned home from work, some of them commuters from London, and among them, walking from a jaunty red sports car, a couple swinging between them a baby in a shallow rush basket. Wexford wondered just how many children under the age of two lived in those flats and small neat houses. Nearly as many as there were adults, he thought, and he stood aside to let pass a girl pushing twins in a wide push-chair.

There was very little more that he could do that night beyond embroiling himself in another discussion with Burden as to the reason why. Burden put forward several strange suggestions. Having previously declared that he couldn't think of a single motive, he now posited that the baby-snatcher was due to have her own baby immunized against whooping cough on the following day. She had read in the newspaper that this could cause brain damage but was too diffident to refuse the immunization, so planned to substitute someone else's baby for her own.

'The trouble with you unimaginative people,' said Wexford, 'is that when you do fantasize you really go crazy. She wants to protect her child from what's something like a one in a million chance of brain damage, but she doesn't mind entrusting him to the care of strangers who might do him far more harm.'

'But the point is she knew they wouldn't do him harm. She'd know that what's happened is exactly what must happen, that he'd be brought to us and then put in the care of the local authority.' Burden waited for some show of enthusiasm and when he didn't get it he went home. For three hours. At eleven that night he was destined to be called out again.

But not on account of Karen Bond.

In normal circumstances Sergeant Willoughby, going off duty, wouldn't have given a second glance at the Ford Transit parked under some overhanging bushes at the foot of Ploughman's Lane. But the sergeant's head, like those of most members of the Mid-Sussex Constabulary, was full of thoughts of missing children. He saw the van as a possible caravan substitute, and his mind went vaguely back to old tales of infants stolen by gypsies. He parked his scooter and went over to investigate.

The young man sitting in the driving seat switched on the ignition, put the van into gear and moved off as fast as he could on a roar of the engine. There was no real danger of his hitting Sergeant Willoughby, nor did that seem to have been his intention, but he passed within a yard or so of him and swung down the lane towards the town.

The nearest phone was in the sergeant's own home in Queen Street, and he went quickly to it.

But the Ford Transit turned out to have had nothing to do with Karen Bond. It was the getaway car for two men who were taking advantage of the absence of a Kingsmarkham stockbroker and his wife to remove a safe from their home.

Ploughman's Lane was Kingsmarkham's millionaire's row, and Stephen Pollard's house, pretentiously named Baron's Keep, by no means the smallest or most modest house in it. It was a nineteen-thirties palace of red brick and leaded lattices and neo-Tudor twisty chimneys. All the windows on the ground floor had stout bars to them, but there were no bars on the french window which led from the largest of the rear bedrooms on to a spacious balcony. When Burden and Loring got there they found signs that two men had climbed up to this balcony, ignored the thief-proof locks on the french window, and cut the glass neatly out of its frame with a glass cutter.

Where the safe had been in the study on the ground floor was now a gaping cavity. This room was said to be a precise replica of some writing room or den or hidey-hole of Mary Queen of Scots in Holyrood Palace, and the safe had been concealed behind a sliding door in the linenfold panelling. The thieves had chipped it out of its niche with a cold chisel and removed it bodily. Burden thought it must have been immensely heavy, which explained the need for having the van nearby.

Although the weather was dry, a long wet spell had only just ended. Deeply indented footprints, one set of a size eight shoe, the other of a size twelve, had ground into the flowerbed under the balcony. These same prints crossed the rear lawn to where there was a gate in the tall wattle fence, and alongside them went parallel grooves about two inches apart.

'I reckon,' said Burden, 'they had a set of those wheels people have for pushing heavy luggage along. That's what they used. The sheer cheek of it!'

Loring shone his torch. 'They rested it down here, sir, in front of the gate. Must have been a bit of a blow when they found their motor gone and they had to keep on wheeling.'

In vain they searched the lane, the ditches and the copse which bordered the lane on one side. They didn't find the safe and no fingerprints were found on the window ledges or in the study at Baron's Keep. The thieves had worn gloves.

'And Big Feet,' said Burden in the morning, 'should have worn snow shoes. There aren't going to be many villains about with great plates of meat like that.'

'I'd think of Lofty Peters first thing,' said Wexford, 'only he's inside.'

'Well, he's not actually. He came out last week. But we were round at his place, knocking him up at midnight and waking all the neighbours, and there was no doubt where he'd been all evening. He was blind drunk, smashed out of his mind. I reckon this lot came down from London. Old Pollard's been shooting his mouth off around the City about his missus's diamonds and this is the outcome.'

'The van was nicked,' said Wexford. 'I've just had a call from the super at Myringham. They found it ditched on the edge of a wood with the licence plates missing.'

'What a lively time we are having,' said Burden, and he looked out of the window at the geraniums on the forecourt and the shops opening, striped awnings gradually being unfurled, shoppers' cars moving in, the July sun spreading a great sheet of light and warmth across the Pomfret Road – and a little figure walking through it in unseasonable black. 'My God,' he said, 'I don't believe it, not another one!'

Wexford got up and came over to the window. The small stout man in the black cassock was now on the forecourt, walking between the geranium tubs. In his arms was a bundle that was undoubtedly a baby. He was carrying the baby very confidently and securely as might be expected in one who so often performed the sacrament of baptism. Wexford watched him in silence, craning out to follow the priest's progress under the overhanging canopy and through the swing doors into the police station.

He said in a distant speculative voice, 'You don't suppose, do you, Mike, that this is the latest craze? I mean, we've had wife-swapping, are we going to have baby-swapping? Maybe it's something that bored young house-wives are going to take up instead of going to evening classes or playing with their deep freezes.'

'Or maybe there's a maniac on the rampage who gets his

kicks from changing them all around and confusing their mums.'

'Musical babes,' said Wexford. 'Come on, let's go down and see.' They descended to the foyer in the lift. 'Good morning, Father. And who might this be?'

The priest in charge of the Catholic church of Our Lady of Loretto was leaning against the long parabola-shaped counter behind which the station sergeant, Sergeant Camb, presided. The sleeping baby in his arms was swathed, indeed tightly cocooned, in a clean pale blue cellular blanket. Only its face, fragile yet healthy-looking, and one hand were exposed. Thick dark lashes rested on the rose-leaf skin, but otherwise the child was fair, eyebrow-less and with fine downy hair as bright as a new copper coin. Holding it with tender firmness, Father Glanville looked round from his conversation with the sergeant to give Wexford a mystified grin, while Polly Davies stroked the baby's tiny fingers with her own forefinger.

'Your guess is as good as mine, Mr Wexford. I went over to the church just before nine and when I came back this little one was on the front steps of the presbytery. My lady help, Mrs Bream, had come in by the back door and hadn't even noticed him.'

'You found him just like that?' said Wexford. 'Just wrapped in that blanket and lying on the doorstep.'

'No indeed. He was wrapped in this blanket inside a cardboard box. The cardboard box,' said Father Glanville, smiling, 'is of the kind one sees in grocery supermarkets. This particular one has printed on it: Smith's Ready Salted

Crisps, Ten Family Packs.' He added rather anxiously, 'I'm afraid I haven't brought it with me.'

Wexford couldn't help laughing. 'Well, don't throw it away. It's very likely a vital piece of evidence.' He came closer to the child who slept on regardless of the talk and the four large alien presences. 'You brought it straight here?'

'I brought *him* straight here,' said Father Glanville with the faintest note of reproof in his voice. Wexford reflected that he ought to have known the priest would never refer to any human soul, however youthful, however unknown and unidentified, as 'it', and then he said:

'I suppose he is a he? Blue blankets don't necessarily denote maleness, do they?'

The three men, for some obscure reason known to none of them, turned their eyes simultaneously on Polly Davies. And she, somehow recognizing that to ascertain gender was her peculiar function, gently took the baby out of Father Glanville's arms, turned away and began unwrapping the blue blanket. The baby woke up and at once began a strenuous crying. Polly re-wrapped the blanket, set the child against her shoulder, her hand pressed against the four-inch wide back.

'This is a little girl, sir.' She put the baby's cheek against her own. 'Sir, don't you think it's Karen Bond? I'm sure it is, it must be.' Her voice had a catch in it. To her own evident horror, there were tears coming into her eyes. 'To think someone just dumped her, someone else's child, on a doorstep, in a cardboard box!'

'Well, the someone couldn't have left her in a better 17

place, could she?' said Wexford with a grin at the priest. 'Come now, Constable Davies, this is no way for a liberated woman to go on. Let us pull ourselves together and go and phone Mrs Bond.'

Trevor and Pippa Bond arrived together, having again been brought to the police station in Susan Rains's car. The young husband was plainly terrified that the child would turn out not to be theirs, that their journey would prove to have been a cruel and vain awakening of hope, and for this reason he had tried to persuaded his wife not to come. But she had come. Nothing could not have kept her away, though she was fuddled and dazed still from Dr Moss's sedatives.

But once she saw the baby the muzziness left her and the glazed look went out of her eyes. She seized her in her arms, crushing her until Karen cried out and struggled with all her nine-week-old energy. Inscrutably, Susan Rains watched the little drama, watched her sister throw the blue blanket on to the floor, shuddering as she did so, watched the tears run down her cheeks on to the baby's head. Pippa began frenetically examining the white frock, the matinée jacket, the minute socks, as if hunting for visible germs.

'Why don't you burn the lot?' said Susan very coolly. 'Then you won't have to worry.'

Trevor Bond said quickly and awkwardly, 'Well, thanks very much, thanks a lot. I'll just see these girls of mine home and then I'll get off to the office. We've got a lot on our plates, always have this time of the year.'

'I'll take them back, Trev,' said Susan. 'You get off to work. And I'll phone Mother.'

'I'd let Dr Moss have a look at Karen if I were you,' said Wexford. 'She seems fine and I'm sure she is, but better be on the safe side.'

They went on their way. Susan Rains walked a little behind the others, already marked for her role as the eternal aunt. Wexford's thoughts went to her nephew, her brother Mark's child, though he didn't know why he should think of him just then, and then to young Ginger, that grass orphan, down in Bystall Lane. He picked up the blanket – young Ginger's blanket? – and examined it, coming to the conclusion at the end of a few minutes' scrutiny of its texture and its label, that it was made of pure wool, had been manufactured in Wales, was old but clean and had been mended in one corner by someone who was no tyro when it came to handling a darning needle. From its honeycombing he picked a quantity of hairs. Most of these were baby hair, very fine red-gold filaments that might (or then again might not) all have come from the same child's scalp, but among them were a few coarser longer hairs that were clearly from a woman's head. A red-headed woman. He was thinking about the two red-headed woman he had encountered during the time Karen was missing, when there came a knock at the door.

Wexford called, 'Come in,' and Sergeant Willougby first put his head round the door, then advanced a little sheepishly into the office. Behind him came Burden.

'The young chap I saw driving that van last night, sir,'

said Willoughby, 'I knew his face was familiar, I knew I'd seen him before. Anyway, I've remembered who he is. Tony Jasper, sir. I'm certain of it.'

'And am I supposed to know who Tony Jasper is?'

Burden said quickly, 'You know his brother. His brother's Paddy Jasper.'

'Paddy Jasper went up north.'

'That's what they said,' said Burden, 'and maybe he did, but his girl friend's back living round here. You know Leilie Somers, he's lived with her on and off for years, ever since she left Stowerton Secondary Modern when she was sixteen.'

'D'you know where she's living?'

'In one of those flats over the shops in Roland Road,' said Burden.

Roland Road was in Stowerton, running behind and parallel to the High Street. Wexford's driver took him and Burden along the High Street to reach it and, looking out of the window, Wexford saw Pippa Bond's mother walking along, shop-window-gazing and pushing a pram that was higher and grander than her daughter's and of a rich dark green colour. Its occupant was presumably her grandson. Mrs Leighton was also dressed in dark green and her dyed hair looked redder than ever.

The car turned left, then right into Roland Road. The row of shops, eight of them, was surmounted by a squat upper floor of aimlessly peaked roofs and, on its façade, a useless adornment of green-painted studs and beams. The block had been put up at approximately the same period as

Baron's Keep, the time which Wexford called the Great Tudor Revival. He remarked to Burden that the whole face of urban and semi-rural Britain would have been changed immeasurably for the better if architects in the third and fourth decades of the century had revived the Georgian instead of the Elizabethan. Think of it, he said, long elegant sash windows instead of poky casements, columns instead of half-timbering and pediments instead of gables. Burden didn't answer him. He had given a push to the door between the newsagent's and the pet food shop, and it gave under his hand and swung inwards.

The passage was rather dark. At the foot of the stairs was a pram from which a young woman was lifting a baby. She turned round as the light fell on her and said:

'Oh, hallo, I was just coming back to shut that. Were you wanting something?'

Burden was inspired. He said, remembering Leilie Somers's character, guessing at her hopes and fears, 'We're looking for Mrs Jasper.'

The girl knew at once whom he meant. 'Leilie's door's the one on the right at the top of the stairs.' The baby on her hip, she parked the pram a little way down the passage, pulled and fastened the cover up over it.

'Do you know if her husband's at home?'

Her reply came guilelessly up to them as they mounted the steep stairs: 'Not unless he's come back. I heard him go out at just after eight this morning.'

At the top there was a door to the left and a door to the right. Burden knocked on the right one, and it was so rapidly opened that it was apparent Leilie Somers had been listening behind it. And she wanted them inside the flat just as fast. Her neighbour was steadily coming up the stairs and Leilie knew better than to let her hear the law introducing itself or see warrant cards flashed. She was a thin little person of twenty-eight or nine with a pinched face and hennaed hair. Throughout her whole youth she had been the mistress of a man who lived by robbery and occasionally by violent crime, and she had herself been in the dock. But she had never come to adopt, as other such women adopt, an attitude of insolence or truculence towards the police. She was always polite, she was always timid, and now as Wexford said, 'So you've moved back to your old stamping ground, Leilie,' she only nodded and smiled nervously and said yes, that was right, she'd moved back, managed to get this flat which was a piece of luck.

'And Paddy with you, I gather.'

'Sometimes,' she said. 'On and off. He's not what you'd call *living* here.'

'What would I call it then? Staying here for his holidays?' Leilie made no answer. The flat seemed to consist of a living room, a bedroom, a lavatory and a kitchen with covered bath in it. They went through to the living room. The furniture in it was ugly and cheap and old but it was very clean and the woodwork and walls were fresh white. The room had been re-decorated perhaps only the week before. There was still a lingering smell of paint. 'He was here last night,' said Wexford. 'He went out around eight this morning. When's he coming back?'

She would be rid of the man if she could be. Wexford had that impression now as he had received it from her once before, years before. Some bond she couldn't break bound her to Paddy Jasper, love or merely habit, but she would be relieved if external circumstances could sever it. Meanwhile, she would be unremittingly loyal.

'What did you want to see him for?'

Two can play at that game, thought Wexford, answering questions with another question. 'Where was he last evening?'

'He was here. He had a couple of pals in playing cards and for a beer.'

'I don't suppose,' said Burden, 'that one of these pals was by any chance his little brother Tony?'

Leilie looked at the rug on the floor, up at the ceiling, then out of the window so intently that it seemed there must be at least Concorde manifesting itself up in the sky if not a flying saucer.

'Come on, Leilie, you know Tony. That nice clean-living young Englishman who did two years for mugging an old lady up in the Smoke.'

She said very quietly, now staring down at her fingers, ''Course I know Tony. I reckon he was here too, I don't know, I was out at my job.' Her voice went up a bit and her chin went up. 'I've got an evening job down the Andromeda. Cloakroom attendant, eight till midnight.'

A sign of the times, was what Wexford called the Andromeda. It was Kingsmarkham's casino, a gambling club in a spruced-up Victorian house out on the Sewingbury

Road. He was going to ask why an evening job, what had happened to her full-time work – for at the time of his last encounter with Leilie she had been a stylist at Mr Nicholas, the hairdresser's – when his eye fixed itself on an object which stood on one end of the mantelpiece. It was a baby's feeding bottle with dregs of milk still in it.

'I didn't know you had a baby, Leilie,' he said.

'He's in the bedroom,' she said, and as if to confirm her words there sounded through the wall a reedy wail which quickly gained in volume. She listened. As the cries grew shrill she smiled and the smile became a laugh, a burst of laughter. Then she bit her lip and said in her usual monotone, 'Paddy and them were here babysitting for me. They were here all evening.'

'I see,' said Wexford. He knew then beyond a doubt that Paddy Jasper had not been there, that his friends had not been there, but that on the other hand they, or some of them including Jasper and his brother, had been up in Ploughman's Lane robbing Baron's Keep. 'I see,' he said again. The baby went on crying, working itself up into a passion of rage or misery. 'Is Paddy the child's father?'

She came the nearest to rudeness she ever had. 'You've no right to ask me that, Mr Wexford. What's it to you?'

No, maybe he had no right, he thought. That ninety-nine out of a hundred policemen would have asked it was no reason why he should. 'It's nothing to me,' he said. 'I'm sorry, Leilie. You'd better go and see to him, hadn't you?'

But at that moment the crying stopped. Leilie Somers sighed. In the flat next door footsteps sounded and a door slammed. Wexford said, 'We'll be back,' and followed Leilie out into the passage. She went into the bedroom and shut herself in.

Burden let them out and closed the front door. 'That's her second child, you know,' he said as they went down the stairs. 'She had a kid by Jasper years ago.'

'Yes, I remember.' Wexford recalled Father Glanville's implied admonition and said carefully, 'Where is he or she now?'

'She's a baby batterer, is Leilie Somers. Didn't you know? No, you wouldn't. The case came up when you were ill and had all that time off.' Wexford didn't much like hearing his month's convalescence after a thrombosis described as 'all that time off' but he said nothing. 'I was amazed,' said Burden severely, 'to hear you apologizing to her as if she were a decent respectable sort of woman. She's a woman who's capable of giving a helpless baby a fractured skull and a broken arm. Those were her kid's injuries. And what did Leilie get? A suspended sentence, a recommendation for psychiatric treatment, all the nonsense.'

'What happened to the little boy?'

'He was adopted,' said Burden. 'He was quite a long time in hospital and then I heard that Leilie had agreed to have him adopted. Best thing for him.'

Wexford nodded. 'Strange, though,' he said. 'She always seems such a gentle meek creature. I can imagine her not knowing how to cope with a child or being a bit too easy-going or not noticing it was ill, say, but baby-battering – it seems so out of character.'

'You're always saying how inconsistent people are. You're always saying people are peculiar and you never can tell what they'll do next.'

'I suppose I am,' said Wexford.

He sent Loring to keep the Roland Road flat under observation, and then he and Burden went to lunch in the police station canteen. Polly Davies came up to Wexford while he was eating his dessert.

'I looked in at Bystall Lane, sir, and saw young Ginger. They said, did we think of making other arrangements for him or were they to keep him for a bit?'

'My God, they haven't had him twenty-four hours yet.'

'That's what I said, sir. Well, I sort of said that. I think they're short-staffed.'

'So are we,' said Wexford. 'Now then, I don't suppose anyone saw Karen Bond being put on that doorstep?'

'I'm afraid not, sir. No one I've spoken to, anyway, and no one's come forward. Mrs Bream who housekeeps for the priest, she says the cardboard box – the Smith's Crisps box, you know – was there when she came at nine only she didn't look at it. She thought it was something someone had left for the father and she was going to take it in once she'd got the kitchen cleared up and his bed made. Father Glanville says he went out at ten to nine and he's positive the box wasn't there then, so someone must have put it there in those ten minutes. It looks like someone who knows their habits, the father's and Mrs Bream's, doesn't it, sir?'

'One of his flock, d'you mean?'

26   'It could be. Why not?'

'If you're right,' said Wexford dryly, 'whoever it was is probably confessing it at this moment and Father Glanville will, of course, have to keep her identity locked in his bosom.'

He went off up to his office to await word from Loring. There, sitting at his desk, thinking, he remembered noticing in Susan Rains's flat, honoured on a little shelf fixed there for the purpose, a plaster statuette of the Virgin with lilies in her arms. The Leightons were perhaps a Catholic family. He was on the point of deciding to go back to Greenhill Court for a further talk with Susan Rains when a phone call from Sergeant Camb announced the arrival of Stephen Pollard.

The stockbroker and his wife had been on holiday in Scotland and had driven all the way back, non-stop, all five hundred and forty miles, starting at six that morning. Wexford had met Pollard once before and remembered him as a choleric person. Now he was tired from the long drive but he still rampaged and shouted with as much misery as Pippa Bond had shown over the loss of her baby. The safe, it appeared, had contained a sapphire and platinum necklace and bracelet, four rings, three cameos and a diamond cross which Pollard said were worth thirty thousand pounds. No, of course no one knew he had a safe in which he kept valuables. Well, he supposed the cleaning woman did and the cleaning woman before her and all of the series of *au pair* girls, and maybe the builders who had painted the outside of the house, and the firm who had put up the bars.

'It's ludicrous,' said Burden when he had gone. 'All that 27 carry-on when it's a dead cert his insurance company'll fork out. He might as well go straight back to Scotland. We're the people who've got the slog and we'll get stick if those villains aren't caught, while it won't make a scrap of difference to him one way or the other. And I'll tell you another thing that's ludicrous,' he said, warming to a resentful theme. 'The ratepayers of Sussex could have the expense of young Ginger's upbringing for eighteen years because his mother's too scared to come and claim him.'

'What shall I do about it? Hold a young wives' meeting and draw them a chalk circle?'

Burden looked bewildered.

'Haven't you ever heard of the Chinese chalk circle and Brecht's *Caucasian Chalk Circle*? You have to draw a circle in chalk on the ground and put the child in it, and of the mothers who claim him the one who can pull him out of the circle is his true mother and may have him.'

'That's all very well,' said Burden after a pause, 'but in this case, it's not mothers who want him, it's he who wants a mother. No one seems to want him.'

'Poor Ginger,' said Wexford, and then the phone rang. It was Loring on his radio to say Paddy Jasper had come into Roland Road and gone up the stairs to Leilie Somers's flat.

By the time Wexford and Burden got there Tony Jasper had arrived as well. The brothers were both tall, heavily built men but Tony's figure still had a youthfully athletic look about it while Paddy had the beginnings of a paunch. Tony's otherwise handsome appearance was ruined by a broken nose which had never been put right and through which he had difficulty in breathing. The repulsive and even sinister air he had was partly due to his always breathing through his mouth. Paddy and he were sitting facing each other at Leilie's living-room table. They were both smoking, the air in the room was thick with smoke, and Tony was dealing a pack of cards. Wexford thought the cards were the inspiration of the moment, hastily fetched out when they heard the knock at the downstairs door.

'Put the cards away, Tone,' said Paddy. 'It's rude to play when we've got company.' He was always polite in a thoroughly offensive way. 'Leilie here,' he said, 'has got something in her head about you wanting to know where I was last evening. Like what sort of time did you have in mind?'

Wexford told him. Paddy smiled. Somehow he managed to make it a paternal smile. He was stopping a few days with Leilie, he said, and his son. He hadn't seen much of his son since the child was born on account of having this good job up north but not a chance of acccommodation for a woman and a kid, no way. So he'd come down for his holidays the previous Saturday and what does he hear but that Leilie's got this evening job up the Andromeda. Well, she'd taken Monday night off to be with him and done an exchange with another girl for Tuesday, but when it got to last night she couldn't very well skive off again so he said not to worry, he'd babysit, him and Tony here, and they'd have some of their old mates round. Johnny Farrow and Pip Monkton, for a beer and a hand of solo.

'Which is what we did, Mr Wexford.'

'Right,' said Tony.

'Leilie put Matthew in his cot and then the boys came round and she got us a bite to eat. She's a good girl is Leilie. She went off to work about half seven, didn't you, love? Then we did the dishes and had our game. Oh, and the lady next door came round to check up if four grown men could look after baby OK, very kind of her, I'm sure. And then at half eleven Pip went off home on account of his missus being the boss round his place, and at quarter past twelve Leilie came back. She got a lift so she was early. That's right, isn't it, love?'

Leilie nodded. 'Except you never did no dishes.'

Wexford kept looking at the man's huge feet which were no longer under the table but splayed out across the cheap bright bit of carpet. He wondered where the shoes were that had made those prints. Burnt, probably. The remains of the safe, once they had blown it open, might be in any pond or river in the Home Counties. Johnny Farrow was a notorious peterman or expert with explosives. He turned to Leilie and asked a question perhaps none of them had expected.

'Who usually looks after the baby when you're working?'

'Julie next door. That girl you were talking to when you came earlier. I used to take him to my mum, my mum lives up Charteris Road, it's not very far, but he started getting funny in the evenings, crying and screaming, and he got worse if I took him out and left him in a strange place.'

Wexford wondered if she was giving him such a detailed

answer to his question because she sometimes left the baby unattended and thought she might be breaking the law. He remembered the other boy, the one with the fractured skull and broken arm, and he hardened towards her. 'Then Mum had to go into hospital, anyway, she only came out yesterday. So Julie said to leave him here and she'd pop in every half hour, and she'd hear him anyway if he cried. You can hear a pin drop through these walls. And Julie never goes out on account of she's got a baby of her own. She's been very good has Julie because I reckon Matthew does cry most evenings, and you can't just leave them to cry, can you?'

'I'm glad to inform you, my dear,' said Paddy with outrageous pomposity, 'that my son did not utter a squeak last evening but was as good as gold,' and on the last word he looked hard at Wexford and stretched his lips into a huge humourless smile.

Julie Lang confirmed that Paddy Jasper, Tony Jasper, Pip Monkton and Johnny Farrow had all been in the flat next door when she called to check on the safety and comfort of Matthew at eight-thirty. She had a key to Leilie's flat but she hadn't used it, knowing Mr Jasper to be there. She wouldn't have dreamt of doing that because it was Mr Jasper's home really, wasn't it? So she had knocked at the door and Mr Jasper had let her in and not been very nice about it actually, and she had felt very awkward especially when he'd said, go in and see for yourself if I'm not to be trusted to look after my own child. He had opened the bedroom door and made her look and she had just glanced at the cot and seen Matthew was all right and sleeping.

'Well, I felt so bad about it,' said Julie Lang, 'that I said to him, perhaps he'd like the key back, and he said, yes, he'd been going to ask me for it as they wouldn't be needing my services any longer, thanks very much. He was quite rude really but I did feel bad about it.'

She had given Paddy Jasper the key. As far as she knew, the four men had remained in the flat with Matthew till Leilie got back at twelve-fifteen. By then, anyway, her husband had come home and they were both in bed asleep. No, she had heard no footsteps on the stairs, not even those of Pip Monkton going home at eleven-thirty. Of course she had had the television on so maybe she wouldn't have heard, but she was positive there hadn't been a sound out of Matthew.

Wexford and Burden went next to the home of Pip Monkton. Johnny Farrow's confirmation of the alibi would amount to very little, for he had a long criminal record for safebreaking, but Monkton had never been convicted of anything, had never even been charged with anything. He was an ex-publican, apparently perfectly respectable, and the only blot on his white innocent life was his known friendship with Farrow with whom he had been at school and whom he had supported and stuck to during Farrow's long prison sentences and periods of poverty-stricken idleness. If Monkton said that the four of them had been together all that evening babysitting in Leilie Somers's flat, Wexford knew he might as well throw up the sponge. The judge, the jury, the court, would believe Pip Monkton just as they would believe Julie Lang.

And Monkton did say it. Looking Wexford straight in the eye (so that the chief inspector knew he must be lying) he declared boldly that he and the Jaspers and Johnny had been in Roland Road, playing solo and drinking beer, until he left for home at half-past eleven. Wexford had him down to the police station and went on asking him about it, but he couldn't break him down. Monkton sounded as if he had learnt by heart what he had to say, and he went on saying it over and over again like a talking bird or a record on which the needle has got stuck.

When it got to six Wexford had himself driven to the Andromeda where the manager, who had an interest in keeping on the right side of the police, answered his questions very promptly. He got back to the station to find Burden and Polly discussing the one relevant piece of information Burden had succeeded in finding out about Monkton – that he had recently had an extension built on to his house. To cover the cost of this he had taken out a second mortgage, but the costs had come to three thousand pounds more than the builder's estimate.

'That'll be about what Monkton's getting for perjury,' said Burden. 'That'll be his share. Tony drove the van. Paddy and Johnny did the job while Monkton covers for them. I imagine they left Leilie's place around nine and got to Ploughman's Lane by a quarter past. They'll have got the safe out in an hour and got to the gate in the fence with it by ten-thirty, which was just about the time Willoughby

33

spotted the van. Tony drove off, ditched the van in Myringham, came back to Stowerton on the last bus, the one that leaves Myringham at ten past eleven and which would have got him to Stowerton High Street by ten to twelve. God knows how the others got that safe back. My guess is that they didn't. They hid it in one of the meadows at the back of Ploughman's Lane and went back for it this morning – with Johnny Farrow's car. Then Johnny blew it. They used the wheels again and Johnny blew it somewhere up on the downs.'

Wexford hadn't spoken for some minutes. Now he said, 'When Leilie Somers was charged with this baby-battering thing, did she plead guilty or not guilty?'

Rather surprised by the apparent irrelevance of this question, Burden said. 'Guilty. There wasn't much evidence offered apart from the doctor's. Leilie pleaded guilty and said something about being tired and strained and not being able to stand it when the baby cried. Damned disgraceful nonsense.'

'Yes, it was damned disgraceful nonsense,' said Wexford quietly, and then he said, 'The walls in those flats are very thin, aren't they? So thin that from one side you can hear a pin drop on the other.' He was silent and meditative for a moment. 'What was Leilie Somers's mother's maiden name?'

'*What?*' said Burden. 'How on earth do you expect me to know a thing like that?'

'I just thought you might. I thought it might be an Irish name, you see. Because Leilie is probably short for Eileen, which is an Irish name. I expect she called herself Leilie when she was too young to pronounce her name properly.'

Burden said with an edge of impatience to his voice, 'Look, do I get to know what all this is leading up to?'

'Sure you do. The arrest of Paddy and Tony Jasper and Johnny Farrow. You can get down to Roland Road and see to it as soon as you like.'

'For God's sake, you know as well as I do we'll never make it stick. We couldn't break Monkton and he'll alibi the lot of them.'

'That'll be OK,' said Wexford laconically. 'Trust me. Believe me, there is no alibi. And now, Polly, you and I will turn our attention to the matter of young Ginger and the Kingsmarkham Chalk Circle.'

Wexford left Polly sitting outside in the car. It was eight o'clock and still light. He rang the bell that had fetched Leilie down that afternoon, and when she didn't come he rang the other. Julie Lang appeared.

'She's upset. I've got her in with me having a cup of tea.'

'I'd like to see her, Mrs Lang, and I'll need to see her alone. I'll go and sit in my car for five minutes and then if she'll . . .'

Leilie Somers's voice from the top of the stairs cut off the end of his sentence. 'You can come up. I'm OK now.'

Wexford climbed the stairs towards her, Julie Lang following him. Leilie stood back to let him pass. She seemed smaller than ever, thinner, meeker, her hennaed hair showing a paler red at the roots, her face white and deeply sad. Julie Lang put her hand on her arm, squeezed it, went off quickly into her own flat. Leilie put the key into the lock of her front door and opened the door and stood looking at the empty neat place, the passage, the open doors into the other rooms, now all made more melancholy by the encroaching twilight. Tears stood in her eyes and she turned her face so that Wexford should not see them fall.

'He's not worth it, Leilie,' said Wexford.

'I know *that*, I know what he's worth. But you won't get me being disloyal to him, Mr Wexford, I shan't say a word.'

'Let's go in and sit down.' He made his way to the table where it was lightest and sat down in the chair Tony Jasper had sat in. 'Where's the baby?'

'With my mum.'

'Rather much for someone who's just come out of hospital, isn't it?' Wexford looked at his watch. 'You're going to be late for work. What time is it you start? Eight-thirty?'

'Eight,' she said. 'I'm not going. I couldn't, not after what's happened to Paddy. Mr Wexford, you might as well go. I'm not going to say anything. If I was Paddy's wife you couldn't make me say anything, and I'm as good as his wife, I've been more to him than most wives'd have been.'

'I know that, Leilie,' said Wexford, 'I know all about that,' and his voice was so loaded with meaning that she stared at him with frightened eyes whose whites shone in the dusk. 'Leilie,' he said, 'when they drew the chalk circle and put the child in it the girl who had brought him up refused to pull him out because she knew she would hurt him. Rather than hurt him she preferred that someone else should have him.'

'I don't know what you're talking about,' she said.

'I think you do. It's not so different from Solomon's judgement of cutting the baby in half. The child's mother wouldn't have that happen, better let the other woman have him. You pleaded guilty in court to crimes against your first son you had never committed. It was Jasper who injured that child, and it was Jasper who got you to take the blame because he knew you would get a light sentence whereas he would get a heavy one. And afterwards you had the baby adopted – not because you didn't love him but because like the chalk circle woman you would rather lose him than have him hurt again. Isn't it true?'

She stared at him. Her head moved, a tiny affirmative bob. Wexford leaned across to the window and opened it. He waved his hand out of the window, withdrew it and closed the casement again. Leilie was crying, making no attempt to dry her tears.

'Were you brought up as a Catholic?' he said.

'I was baptized,' she said in a voice not much above a whisper. 'Mum's a Catholic. Her and Dad, they got married in Galway where Mum comes from, and Dad had to promise to bring the kids up Catholic.' A sob caught her throat. 'I haven't been to mass for years. Mr Wexford, please go away now and leave me alone. I just want to be left alone.'

He said, 'I'm sorry to hear you say that because I've got a visitor for you, and he'll certainly be staying the night.' He switched on lights, the living-room light, the light in the hall and one over the top of the door, and then he opened the door and Polly Davies walked in with young Ginger in her arms.

Leilie blinked at the light. She closed her eyes and lowered her head, and then she lifted it and opened her eyes and made a sort of bound for Polly, nearly knocking Wexford over. But she didn't snatch Ginger. She stood trembling, looking at Polly, her hands moving slowly forward until, with an extreme gentle tenderness, they closed over and caressed the baby's downy red-gold head.

'Matthew,' she said. 'Matthew.'

The baby lay in Leilie's lap. He had whimpered a little at first, but now he lay quiet and relaxed, gripping one of her fingers, and for the first time in their acquaintance Wexford saw him smile. It was a beautiful spontaneous smile of happiness at being home again with Mother.

'You're going to tell me all about it, aren't you, Leilie?' said Wexford.

She was transformed. He had never seen her so animated, so high-spirited. She was giggly with joy so that Matthew, sensing her mood, gurgled in response, and she hugged him again, calling him her lovely lovely sweetheart, her precious boy.

'Come on now, Leilie,' said Wexford, 'you've got him back without the least trouble to yourself which is more than you damn' well deserve. Now you can give an account of yourself.'

'I don't know where to start,' said Leslie, giggling.

'At the beginning, whenever that is.'

'Well, the beginning,' said Leilie, 'I reckon was when Patrick, my first boy, was adopted.' She had stopped laughing and a little of the old melancholy had come back into her face. 'That was four years ago. Paddy went off up north and after a bit he wrote and said would I join him, and I don't know why I said yes, I reckon I always do say yes to Paddy, and there didn't seem anything else, there didn't seem any future. It was all right with Paddy for a bit, and then a couple of years back he got this other girl. I sort of pretended I didn't know about it. I thought he'd get tired of her, but he didn't and I was lonely, I was so lonely. I didn't know a soul up there but Paddy, not like I could talk to, and he'd go away for weeks on end. I sort of took to going out with other fellas, anyone, I didn't care, just for the company.' She paused, shifted Matthew on her knees. 'When I knew I was pregnant I told Paddy I wasn't having the baby up there, I was going home to Mum. But he said to stay and he wouldn't see the other girl, and I did stay till after Matthew was born, and then I knew he was carrying on again so I came back here and Mum got me this flat. I know what you're going to say, Mr Wexford!'

'I wasn't going to say a word.'

'You were thinking it. So what? It's true. I couldn't tell you who Matthew's father is, I don't know. It might be Paddy, it might be one of half a dozen.' Her expression had grown fierce. She almost glared at him. 'And I'm glad I don't know, I'm glad. It makes him more mine. I never went out with any other fella but Paddy till he drove me to it.'

'All right,' said Wexford, 'all right. So you lived here with Matthew and you had your job at the Andromeda and then Paddy wrote to say he was coming down, and on Saturday he did come. And you took Monday evening off work to be with him and exchanged your Tuesday turn with another girl – and so we come to Wednesday, yesterday.'

Leilie sighed. She didn't seem unhappy, only rueful. 'Paddy said he'd babysit. He said he'd asked Tony over and Johnny and a fella called Pip Monkton, and they'd be in all evening. I said he wasn't to bother, I could take Matthew next door into Julie's, and Paddy got mad at me and said Julie was an interfering bitch and didn't I trust him to look after his own child? Well, that was it, I didn't, I kept remembering what he'd done to Patrick, and that was because Patrick cried. Paddy used to go crazy when he cried, I used to think he'd kill him, and when I tried to stop him he nearly killed me. And, you see, Mr Wexford, Matthew'd got into this way of crying in the evenings. They said at the clinic some babies cry at night and some in the evenings and it's hard to know why, but they all grow out of it. I knew Matthew'd start screaming about eight and I thought, my God, what'll Paddy do? He gets in a rage, he doesn't know what he's doing, and Tony wouldn't stop him, he's scared of him like they all are, Paddy's so big. Well, I got in a real state. Mum'd come out of hospital that morning, she'd had a major op, so I couldn't take him there and go back there myself and hide from Paddy, and I couldn't take him to work. I did once and they made a hell of a fuss. I just couldn't see any way out of it.

'Paddy went out about eleven. He never said where he was going and I didn't ask. Anyway, I went out too, carrying Matthew in the baby carrier, and I just walked about thinking. I reckon I must have walked miles, worrying about it and wondering what to do and imagining all sorts of things, you know how you do. I'd been feeding Matthew myself and I'm still giving him one feed a day, so I took him into a field and fed him under a hedge, and after that I walked a bit more.

'Well, I was coming back along the Stowerton Road. I knew I'd have to go home on account of Matthew was wet and he'd soon be hungry again, and then I saw this pram. I knew who it belonged to, I'd seen it there before and I'd seen this girl lift her baby out of it. I mean, I didn't know her name or anything but I'd talked to her once queuing for the check-out in the Tesco, and we'd got talking about our babies and she said hers never cried except sometimes for a feed in the night. She was such a good baby, they never got a peep out of her all day and all evening. She was a bit younger than Matthew but it was funny, they looked a bit alike and they'd got just the same colour hair.

'That was what gave me the idea, them having the same colour hair. I know I was mad, Mr Wexford, I know that now. I was crazy, but you don't know how scared of Paddy I was. I went over to that pram and I bent over it. I unhooked the cat net and took the other baby out and put Matthew in.'

Until now quite silent in her corner, Polly Davies gave a 41 suppressed exclamation. Wexford drew in his breath, shaking his head.

'It's interesting,' he said, and his voice was frosty, 'how I supposed at first that whoever had taken Karen Bond wanted her and wished to be rid of her own child. Now it looks as if the reverse was true. It looks as if she didn't at all mind sacrificing Karen for her own child's safety.'

Leilie said passionately, 'That's not true!'

'No, perhaps it isn't, I believe you did have second thoughts. Go on.'

'I put Matthew in the pram. I knew he'd be all right, I knew no one'd hurt him, but it went to my heart when he started to cry.'

'Weren't you afraid someone would see you?' asked Polly.

'I wouldn't have cared if they had. Don't you see? I was past caring for any of that. If I'd been seen I wouldn't have had to go home, I'd have lost my job, but they wouldn't have taken Matthew from me, would they? No one saw me. Did you say her name was Karen? Well, I took Karen home and I fed her and bathed her. No one can say I didn't look after her like she was my own.'

'Except for delivering her into the hands of that ravening wolf, Paddy Jasper,' said Wexford unpleasantly.

She shivered a little but otherwise she took no notice. 'Paddy came in at six with Tony. The baby was in Matthew's cot by then. All you could see was its red hair like Matthew's. I remembered what that girl had said about her never crying in the evenings, and I thought, I prayed, don't cry tonight, don't cry because you're in a strange place.' Leilie lifted her head and began to speak more rapidly. 'I cooked egg and chips for the lot of them and I went out at half seven. I got back at a quarter past twelve and she was OK, she was fast asleep and she hadn't cried at all.'

Wexford said softly, 'Haven't you forgotten something, Leilie?'

Her eyes darted over him. He fancied she had grown a little paler. She picked up Matthew and held him closely against her. 'Well, the next day,' she said. 'Today. Paddy went off out early so I thought about getting the baby back. I thought of taking her to the priest. I knew about the priest, when he went out and when the lady cleaner came, I knew about it from Mum. So I got on the bus to Kingsmarkham and just by the bus stop's a shop where they'd put all their boxes out on the pavement for the dustmen. I took a box and put the baby in and left her on the doorstep of the priest's house. But I didn't know how I was going to get Matthew back, I thought I'd never get him back.

'And then you came. I said Matthew was in the bedroom and just then Julie's baby started crying and you thought it was Matthew. I couldn't help laughing, though I felt I was going to pieces, I was being torn apart. And that's all, that's everything, and now you can charge me with whatever it is I've done.'

'But you've forgotten something, Leilie.'

'I don't know what you mean,' she said.

'Of course you do. Why d'you think I had Paddy and

Tony and Johnny Farrow arrested even though Pip Monkton had given them all a cast-iron alibi? How do you think I know Pip will break down and tell me that tale of his was all moonshine and tell me as well just where the contents of that safe are now? I had a little talk with the management of the Andromeda this afternoon, Leilie.'

She gave him a stony stare.

'You've got the sack, haven't you?' he said. 'Work out your notice till the end of next week or go now. They were bound to catch you out.'

'If you know all about it, Mr Wexford, why ask?'

'Because I want you to say yes.'

She whispered something to the baby, but the baby had fallen asleep.

'If you won't tell me, I shall tell you,' said Wexford, 'and if I get it wrong you can stop me. I'm going to tell you about those second thoughts you had, Leilie. You went off to work like you said but you weren't easy in your mind. You kept thinking about that baby, that other baby, that good baby that never cried in the evenings. But maybe the reason she didn't cry was that she was usually in her own bed, safe and secure in her own home with her own mother, maybe it'd be different if she woke up to find herself in a strange place. So you started worrying. You ran around that glorified ladies' loo where you work, wiping the basins and filling the towel machines and taking your ten pence tips, but you were going off your head with worry about that other baby. You kept thinking of her crying and what that animal Paddy Jasper might do to her if she cried, punch her with his great fists perhaps or bash her head against the wall. And then you knew you hadn't done anything so clever after all in swapping Matthew for her, because you're a kind loving woman at heart, Leilie, though you're a fool, and you were as worried about her as you'd have been about him.'

'And you're a devil,' whispered Leilie, staring at him as if he had supernatural powers. 'How d'you know what I thought?'

'I just know,' said Wexford. 'I know what you thought and I know what you did. When it got to half-past nine you couldn't stand it any longer. You put on your coat and ran out to catch the nine-thirty-five bus and you were home, walking up those stairs, by five to ten. There were lights on in the flat. You let yourself in and went straight into the bedroom, and Karen was in there, safe and sound and fast asleep.'

Leilie smiled a little. A ghost of a smile of happy recollection crossed her face and was gone. 'I don't know how you know,' she said, 'but yes, she was OK and asleep, and oh God, the relief of it. I'd been picturing her lying there with blood on her and I don't know what.'

'So all you had to do then was explain to Paddy why you'd come home.'

'I told him I felt ill,' said Leilie carefully. 'I said I felt rotten and I'd got one of my migraines coming.'

'No, you didn't. He wasn't there.'

'What d'you mean, wasn't there? He was there! Him and Tony and Pip and Johnny, they were in here playing cards. I 45 said to Paddy, I feel rotten, I had to come home. I'm going to have a lay-down, I said, and I went into the bedroom and laid down.'

'Leilie, when you came in the flat was empty. You know it was empty. You know Pip Monkton's lying and you know his story won't stand up for two seconds once you tell the truth that at *five to ten this flat was empty*. Listen to me, Leilie. Paddy will go away for quite a long time over this business. It'll be a chance for you and young Ginger – er, Matthew, to make a new life. You don't want him round you for ever, do you? Ruining your life, beating up your kids? Do you, Leilie?'

She lifted the baby in her arms. She walked the length of the room and half back again as if he were restless and needed soothing instead of peacefully asleep. In front of Wexford she stood still, looking at him, and he got to his feet.

'We'll come and fetch you in the morning, Leilie,' he said, 'and take you to the police station where I'll want you to make a statement. Maybe two statements. One about taking Karen and one about Paddy not being here when you came back last night.'

'I won't say a thing about that,' she said.

'It might be that we wouldn't proceed with any charge against you for taking Karen.'

'I don't care about that!'

He hated doing it. He knew he had to. 'A woman who knew what you knew about Paddy and who still exposed a child to him, someone else's child – how'll that sound in court, Leilie? When they know you're living with Paddy again? And when they hear your record?'

Her face had gone white and she clasped Matthew against her. 'They wouldn't take him away from me? They wouldn't make a what-d'you-call-it?'

'A care order? They might.'

'Oh God, oh God. I promised myself I'd stick by Paddy all my life . . .'

'Romantic promises, Leilie, they haven't much to do with real life.' Wexford moved a little away from her. He went to the window. It was quite dark outside now. 'They told me at the Andromeda that you came back at half-past ten. You'd been away an hour and there had been complaints so they sacked you.'

She said feverishly, 'I did go back. I told Paddy I felt better, I . . .'

'All in the space of five minutes? Or ten at the most? You were quickly ill and well, Leilie. Shall I tell you why you went back, shall I tell you the only circumstances in which you'd have dared go back? You didn't want to lose your job but you were more afraid of what Paddy might do to the baby. If Paddy had been there the one thing you wouldn't have done is go back. Because he wasn't there you went back with a light heart. You believed he could only get in again when you were there to let him in. You didn't know then that he had a key, they key he had taken from Julie Lang.'

She spoke at last the word he had been waiting for. 'Yes.' She nodded. 'Yes, it's true. If I'd known he had that key,' she said, and she shivered, 'I'd no more have gone and left that baby there than I'd have left it in the lion house at the zoo.'

'We'll be on our way,' he said. 'Come along, Constable Davies. See you in the morning, Leilie.'

Still holding Matthew, she came up to him just as he reached the door and laid a hand on his sleeve. 'I've been thinking about what you said, Mr Wexford,' she said, 'and I don't think I'd be able to pull anybody's baby, *any* baby, out of that circle.'

May and June

Their parents named them May and June because their birthdays occurred in those months. A third sister, an April child, had been christened Avril but she had died. May was like the time of year in which she had been born, changeable, chilly and warm by turns, sullen yet able to know and show a loveliness that couldn't last.

In the nineteen thirties, when May was in her twenties, it was still important to get one's daughters well married, and though Mrs Thrace had no anxieties on that head for sunny June, she was less sanguine with regard to May. Her elder daughter was neither pretty nor graceful nor clever, and no man had ever looked at her twice. June, of course, had a string of admirers. Then May met a young lawyer at a *thé dansant*. His name was Walter Symonds, he was extremely good looking, his father was wealthy and made him a generous allowance, and there was no doubt he belonged in a higher social class than that of the Thraces. May fell passionately in love with him, but no one was more surprised than she when he asked her to marry him.

The intensity of her passion frightened Mrs Thrace. It wasn't quite nice. The expression on her face while she awaited the coming of her fiancé, her ardour when she greeted him, the hunger in her eyes – that sort of thing was all very well in the cinema, but unsuitable for a civil servant's daughter in a genteel suburb.

Briefly, she had become almost beautiful. 'I'm going to marry him,' she said when warned. 'He wants me to love him, doesn't he? He loves me. Why shouldn't I show my love?'

June, who was clever as well as pretty, was away at college training to be a schoolteacher. It had been considered wiser, long before Walter Symonds was thought of, to keep May at home. She had no particular aptitude for anything and she was useful to her mother about the house. Now, of course, it turned out that she had an aptitude for catching a rich, handsome and successful husband. Then, a month before the wedding, June came home for the summer holidays.

It was all very unfortunate, Mrs Thrace said over and over again. If Walter Symonds had jilted May for some unknown girl, they would have been bitterly indignant, enraged even, and Mr Thrace would have felt old-fashioned longings to apply a horsewhip. But what could anyone say or do when he transferred his affections from the elder daughter to the younger?

May screamed and sobbed and tried to attack June with a knife. 'We're all terribly sorry for you, my darling,' said Mrs Thrace, 'but what can anyone do? You wouldn't marry a man who doesn't love you, would you?'

'He does love me, he does! It's just because she's pretty. She's cast a spell on him. I wish she was dead and then he'd love me again.'

'You mustn't say that, May. It's all very cruel, but you have to face the fact that he's changed his mind. Isn't it better to find out now than later?'

'I would have had him,' said May.

Mrs Thrace blushed. She was shocked to the core.

'I shall never marry now,' said May. 'She's ruined my life and I shall never have anything ever again.'

Walter and June were married, and Walter's father bought them a big house in Surrey. May stayed at home, being useful to her mother. The war came. Walter went straight into the army, became a captain, a major, finally a colonel. May also went into the army, where she remained a private for five years, working in some catering department. After that, there was nothing for it but to go home to her parents once more.

She never forgave her sister.

'She stole my husband,' she said to her mother.

'He wasn't your husband, May.'

'As good as. You wouldn't forgive a thief who came into your house and stole the most precious thing you had or were likely to have.'

'We're told to forgive those who trespass against us, as we hope to be forgiven.'

'I'm not religious,' said May, and on those occasions when the Symondses came to the Thrace home she took care to be out of it. But she knew all about them – all, that is, except one thing.

Mr and Mrs Thrace were most careful never to speak of

June in her presence, so May listened outside the door, and she secretly read all June's letters to her mother. Whenever Walter's name was spoken or mentioned in a letter, she winced and shivered with the pain of it. She knew that they had moved to a much larger house, that they were building up a collection of furniture and pictures. She knew where they went for their holidays and what friends they entertained. But what she was never able to discover was how Walter felt about June. Had he ever really loved her? Had he repented of his choice? May thought that perhaps, after the first flush of infatuation was over, he had come to long for his former love as much as she longed for him. Since she never saw them she could never know, for, however he might feel, Walter couldn't leave June. When you have done what he had done you can't change again. You have to stick it out till death.

It comforted her, it was perhaps the only thing that kept her going, to convince herself that Walter regretted his bargain. If there had been children, what the Victorians called pledges of love . . .

Sometimes, after a letter had come from June, May would see her mother looked particularly pleased and satisfied. And then, shaking with dread, she would read the letter, terrified to find that June was pregnant. But Mrs Thrace's pleasure and satisfaction must have come from some other source, from some account of Walter's latest coup in court or June's latest party, for no children came and now June was past forty.

Trained for nothing, May worked as canteen supervisor

in a woman's hostel. She continued to live at home until her parents died. Their deaths took place within six months, Mrs Thrace dying in March and her widower in August. And that was how it happened that May saw Walter again.

At the time of her mother's cremation, May was ill with a virus infection and unable to attend. But she had no way of avoiding her father's funeral. When she saw Walter come into the church a faintness seized her and she huddled against the pew rail, trembling. She covered her face with her hands to make it seem as if she were praying, and when at last she took them away he was beside her. He took her hand and looked into her face. May's eyes met his which were as blue and compelling as ever, and she saw with anguish that he had lost none of his looks but that they had become only more distinguished. She would have liked to die then, holding his hand and gazing into his face.

'Won't you come and speak to your sister, May?' said Walter in the rich deep voice which charmed juries, struck terror into the hearts of witnesses and won women. 'Shall we let bygones be bygones on this very sad day?'

May shivered. She withdrew her hand and marched to the back of the church. She placed herself as far away from June as she could get, but not too far to observe that it was June who took Walter's arm as they left and not Walter June's, June who looked up to Walter for comfort while his face remained grave and still, June who clung to him while he merely permitted the clinging. It couldn't be that he was behaving like that because she, May, was there. He must hate and despite June as she, with all her heart, hated and   53 despised her still.

But it was at a funeral that they were reconciled. May learnt of Walter's death through reading an announcement of it in a newspaper. And the pain of it was as great as that she had suffered when her mother had told her he wanted to marry June. She sent flowers, an enormous wreath of snow-white roses that cost her half a week's wages. And of course she would go to the funeral, whether June wanted her there or not.

Apparently June did want her. Perhaps she thought the roses were for the living bereaved and not for the dead. She came up to May and put her arms round her, laying her head against her sister's shoulder in misery and despair. May broke their long silence.

'Now you know what it's like to lose him,' she said.

'Oh, May, May, don't be cruel to me now! Don't hold that against me now. Be kind to me now, I've nothing left.'

So May sat beside June, and after the funeral she went back to the house where June had lived with Walter. In saying she had nothing left, June had presumably been referring to emotional rather than material goods. Apart from certain stately homes she had visited on tours, May had never seen anything like the interior of that house.

'I'm going to retire next month,' she said, 'and then I'll be living in what they call a flatlet – one room and a kitchen.'

Two days later there came a letter from June.

'Dearest May, Don't be angry with me for calling you that. You have always been one of my dearest, in spite of what I did and in spite of your hatred of me. I can't be sorry for what I did because so much happiness came of it for me, but I am truly, deeply, sorry that you were the one to suffer. And now, dear May, I want to try to make up to you for what I did, though I know I can never really do that, not now, not after so long. You said you were going to retire and wouldn't be living very comfortably. Will you come and live with me? You can have as many rooms in this house as you want, you are welcome to share everything with me. You will know what I mean when I say I feel that would be just. Please make me happy by saying you forgive me and will come. Always your loving sister, June.'

What did the trick was June saying it would be just. Yes, it would be justice if May could now have some of those good things which were hers by right and which June had stolen from her along with her man. She waited a week before replying and then she wrote: 'Dear June, What you suggest seems a good idea. I have thought about it and I will make my home with you. I have very little personal property, so moving will not be a great headache. Let me know when you want me to come. It is raining again here and very cold. Yours, May.' There was nothing, however, in the letter about forgiveness.

And yet May, sharing June's house, was almost prepared to forgive. For she was learning at last what June's married life had been.

'You can talk about him if you want to,' she had said hungrily on their first evening together. 'If it's going to relieve your feelings, I don't mind.'

'What is there to say except that we were married for   55

forty years and now he's dead?'

'You could show me some of the things he gave you.' May picked up ornaments, gazed at pictures. 'Did he give you that? What about this?'

'They weren't presents. I bought them or he did.'

May couldn't help getting excited. 'I wonder you're not afraid of burglars. This is a proper Aladdin's Cave. Have you got lots of jewellery too?'

'Not much,' said June uncomfortably.

May's eyes were on June's engagement ring, a poor thing of diamond chips in nine carat gold, far less expensive than the ring Walter had given his first love. Of course she had kept hers and Walter, though well off even then, hadn't been rich enough to buy a second magnificent ring within six months of the first. But later, surely . . . ?

'I should have thought you'd have an eternity ring.'

'Marriage doesn't last for eternity,' said June. 'Let's not talk about it any more.'

May could tell she didn't like talking about it. Soon she shied at mentioning Walter's name and she put away the photographs of him which had stood on the piano and the drawing room mantelpiece. May wondered if Walter had ever written any letters to his wife. They had seldom been parted, of course, but it would be strange if June had received no letter from him in forty years. The first time June went out alone, May tried to open her desk. It was locked. The drawers of June's dressing table disclosed a couple of birthday cards with 'Love from Walter' scrawled hastily on them, and the only other written message from her husband June had considered worth keeping May found tucked into a cookery book in the kitchen. It was a note written on the back of a bill, and it read: 'Baker called. I ordered large white for Saturday.'

That night May reread the two letters she had received from Walter during their engagement. Each began, 'Dearest May.' She hadn't looked at them for forty years – she hadn't dared – but now she read them with calm satisfaction. 'Dearest May, This is the first love letter I have ever written. If it isn't much good you must put it down to lack of practice. I miss you a lot and rather wish I hadn't told my parents I would come on this holiday with them . . .' 'Dearest May, Thanks for both your letters. Sorry I've taken so long to reply but I feel a bit nervous that my letters don't match up to yours. Still, with luck, we soon shan't have to write to each other because we shan't be separated. I wish you were here with me . . .' Poor Walter had been reticent and shy, unable to express his feelings on paper or by word of mouth. But at least he had written love letters to her and not notes about loaves of bread. May decided to start wearing her engagement ring again – on her little finger of course because she could no longer get it over the knuckle of her ring finger. If June noticed she didn't remark on it.

'Was it you or Walter who didn't want children?' May asked.

'Children just didn't come.'

'Walter *must* have wanted them. When he was engaged to me we talked of having three.'

June looked upset but May could have talked of Walter all day long.

'He was only sixty-five,' she said. 'That's young to die these days. You never told me what he died of.'

'Cancer,' said June. 'They operated but he never regained consciousness.'

'Just like mother,' said May. Suppose June had had cancer and had died, what would have happened then? Remembering Walter's tender look and strong handclasp at her father's funeral, May thought he would have married her. She twisted the ring on her little finger. 'You were almost like a second wife, weren't you? It must be a difficult position.'

'I'd much rather not talk about it,' said June, and with her handkerchief to her eyes she left the room.

May was happy. For the first time in forty years she was happy. She busied herself about the house, caring for June's things, dusting and polishing, pausing to look at a picture and reflecting that Walter must often have looked at it. Sometimes she imagined him sitting in his chair or standing by that window, his heart full of regret for what he might have had. And she thought now, while he had been longing for her she, far away, had been crying for him. She never cried now, though June did.

'I'm an old fool, I can't help giving way. You're strong, May, but I'm weak and I miss him so.'

'Didn't I miss him?'

'He was always fond of you. It upset him a lot to think you were unhappy. He often talked about you.' June looked at her piteously. 'You have forgiven me, haven't you, May?'

'As a matter of fact, I have,' said May. She was a little surprised at herself but, yes, she had forgiven June. 'I think you've been punished for what you did.' A loveless marriage, a husband who talked constantly of another woman . . .

'I've been punished,' said June and she put her arms round May's neck.

The strong and the weak. May remembered those words when a movement downstairs woke her in the night. She heard footsteps and the sound of a door being forced. It was the burglar she feared and had warned June about, but June would be cowering in her room now, incapable of taking any action.

May put on her dressing gown and went stealthily along the passage to June's room. The bed was empty. She looked out of the window, and the moonlight showed her a car parked on the gravel drive that led down to the lane. A yellower, stronger light streamed from the drawing room window. A shiver of fear went through her, but she knew she must be strong.

Before she reached the head of the stairs she heard a violent crash as of something heavy yet brittle hurled against a wall. There was a cry from below, footsteps running. May got to the stairs in time to see a slight figure rush across the hall and slam the front door behind him. The car started up.

In his wake he had left a thin trail of blood. May followed the blood trail into the drawing room. June stood by her 59 desk which had been torn open and all its contents scattered on to the table. She was trembling, tearful and laughing with shaky hysteria, pointing to the shards of cut glass that lay everywhere.

'I threw the decanter at him. I hit him and it cut his head and he ran.'

May went up to her. Are you all right?'

'He didn't touch me. He pointed that gun at me when I came in, but I didn't care. I couldn't bear to see him searching my desk, getting at all my private things. Wasn't I brave? He didn't get away with anything but a few bits of silver. I hit him and he heard you coming and he panicked. Wasn't I brave, May?'

But May wasn't listening. She was reading the letter which lay open and exposed on top of the paper the burglar had pulled out of the desk. Walter's bold handwriting leapt at her, weakened though it was, enfeebled by his last illness. 'My darling love, It is only a moment since you walked out of the ward, but nevertheless I must write to you. I can't resist an impulse to write now and tell you how happy you have made me in all the years we have been together. If the worst comes to the worst, my darling, and I don't survive the operation, I want you to know you are the only woman I have ever loved . . .'

'I wouldn't have thought I'd have had the courage,' said June, 'but perhaps the gun wasn't loaded. He was only a boy. Would you call the police, please, May?'

'Yes,' said May. She picked up the gun.

The police arrived within fifteen minutes. They brought a

doctor with them, but June was already dead, shot through the heart at close range.

'We'll get him, Miss Thrace, don't you worry,' said the inspector.

'It was a pity you touched the gun, though. Did it without thinking, I suppose?'

'It was the shock,' said May. 'I've never had a shock like that, not since I was a girl.'

A Note on Ruth Rendell

Ruth Rendell is crime fiction at its very best. Her first novel, *From Doon With Death*, appeared in 1964, and since then her reputation and readership have grown steadily with each new book. She has received ten major awards for her work: three Edgars from the Mystery Writers of America; the Crime Writers' Gold Dagger Award for 1976's best crime novel for *A Demon In My View*; the Arts Council National Book Award for Genre Fiction in 1981 for *Lake of Darkness*; the Crime Writers' Gold Dagger Award for 1986's best crime novel for *Live Flesh*; in 1987 the Crime Writers' Gold Dagger Award for *A Fatal Inversion* and in 1991 the same award for *King Solomon's Carpet*, both written under the name of Barbara Vine; the *Sunday Times* Literary Award in 1990; and in 1991 the Crime Writers' Cartier Diamond Award for outstanding contribution to the genre. Her books are translated into 21 languages.